Victorian Tales

The Fabulous Flyer

This second edition first published 2016 by
Bloomsbury Education, an imprint of Bloomsbury Publishing Plc
50 Bedford Square, London, WC1B 3DP

www.bloomsbury.com

First published in 2012 by A & C Black Limited.

Bloomsbury is a registered trademark of Bloomsbury Publishing Plc

A CIP catalogue for this book is available from the British Library

ISBN: 978 1 4729 3982 1 (paperback)

Printed and Bound by CPI Group (UK) Ltd, Croydon CR0 4YY

1 3 5 7 9 10 8 6 4 2

TERRY DEARY

Victorian Tales

The Fabulous Flyer

Inside illustrations by
Helen Flook

BLOOMSBURY EDUCATION
AN IMPRINT OF BLOOMSBURY
LONDON OXFORD NEW YORK NEW DELHI SYDNEY

Chapter 1

The shuffling, snuffling and scuffling of the rats woke Marie. She was used to sharing the hay loft with her twitching-whiskered, squeaking, sleek furred friends. But this morning they were racing through the hay and running away from something.

5

The girl stretched and yawned and scratched. A soft breath of air ruffled her hair. Someone must have opened the barn door beneath her. But that someone had opened the creaking leather hinges gently so they didn't wake her. Only the running rats had heard it.

Marie rose to her feet and brushed hay from her plain grey dress. She tiptoed to the trapdoor and looked down to the barn floor below. The early morning light spilled through the open door.

A man crept over the floor, quite silent in his soft leather boots. He was button-burstingly fat and his top hat was as tall as a clown's shoe is long.

But his face was not the face of a clown. His face was purple-red and his dark eyes would have looked good on a bat. He stretched out a hand and grasped the

creamy linen cloth that was stretched tight over a wooden frame. "Nice," he muttered, and his bat eyes glittered.

"No," Marie gasped.

He looked up, as guilty as a dog caught with a stolen sausage. He saw the girl and his mouth turned down in a sneer.

Marie had seen greater hate in faces when she begged on the Paris streets. She wasn't afraid.

7

"Don't touch it," she said.

The man placed his hands on his hips and looked up. "Mr Giffard owes me twenty francs for rent on this barn. He hasn't paid so he can get out." The man waved a hand at the linen. "I'll sell this cloth to get my money."

"I'll give you the money," Marie said. "Give me a day, Mr Herbert, and I will pay you twenty – no, twenty-five francs. I promise."

The man's mean mouth fell open. "What? Where would a street urchin like you get twenty-five francs? You've never seen twenty-five francs in your whole miserable life."

"Henri Giffard is going to be famous... rich and famous. I'll show you," she said, and scrambled down the ladder from the loft. She dropped, mouse-light, to the floor beside Mr Herbert. His gold watch and chain glittered in the light from the dove-grey sky. She licked her lips. It would be so easy for her thin fingers to steal the watch and chain. She'd done it a dozen times before. Instead she stood up straight and looked the man in the eye.

She waved a piece of paper in Herbert's face. "See?"

"What does it say?" he grumbled.

"Read it," she said.

"*You* read it," he replied.

The girl's thin face split in a grin. "I can't read."

The man scowled. "Neither can I."

Marie sighed. "It's a poster," she explained.

"I can see that."

"It says Mr Henri Giffard will fly the first powered air machine in history," she told the man.

He snorted. "People have been flying balloons for as long as I can remember. Nothing new about that."

"No-o," she groaned. She let the poster flutter to the floor as her fingers twitched to take his gleaming watch.

"Mr Giffard says hot air balloons are like soap bubbles – they are blown by the wind. They float, they don't fly. He's invented this thing he calls an 'airship'. Mr Giffard will use steam power to make his airship fly anywhere in France... anywhere in the world," she said proudly.

"No he won't," Herbert said.

"He won't?"

The man leaned forward till Marie could smell the perfumed wax on his beard.

"He won't. Because I am going to take the linen off his balloon and sell it. Now get out of my way, urchin."

Chapter 2

Marie jumped in front of the large man. "You'll get your twenty francs," she cried. "When Mr Giffard flies his steam-powered airship, the people of Paris will make him their hero. These posters are all over the city."

"I don't want a hero in my barn. I want to rent it out to a man who can pay me money."

"No, no, wait. I will be going round the crowd and

collecting money. There will be thousands there. I bet I get a hundred francs at least. I can easily pay you twenty-five."

The man twisted his waxed moustache. "Then you can easily pay me fifty," he said and his weasel eyes sparkled bright as his watch chain.

"Fifty?"

"Fifty... or I tear this balloon apart now."

"Ohhhh," Marie moaned. "Fifty it is."

The man stepped over the tangle of ropes that lay on the barn floor and waddled to the door.

"Before darkness falls tonight, or Henri Giffard will come back to find the lock has changed. You have twelve hours." He jabbed a finger, fat as a sausage, towards the girl. "And you will be back sleeping in the gutter where he found you."

She gave him her sweetest smile.

"Twelve hours, Mr Herbert. You are the kindest man in the whole of this barn."

The man grunted and pushed his way through the door. The girl stuck out a tongue at his back.

She opened the lid of a small metal box. Mr Giffard had made it for her to put her bread and cheese in, and keep out the rats. Marie liked the rats... but they could find their own food. Every day she went around to the bakers to beg for yesterday's old bread. She sat on the floor to chew and shoo away the whisker-twitching rats.

When the barn door opened again Henri Giffard walked in. He was thin and worried-looking, and the soot of the railway yard had turned his pale skin grey as the morning clouds. His suit was getting old, and his shirt was as thin as rainwater.

Marie jumped to her feet. "Are you ready to go, Mr Giffard?" she asked.

He frowned and waved a bony hand. "No, no, child. It's too windy. The airship will fly against a light breeze but not a wind like this."

"But you have to," she groaned. "You have to fly in the next twelve hours."

"Why?"

"Because... we had the posters made... people will be coming out to watch," she said. The girl had made herself the inventor's guardian, and didn't want to worry him with the threats from the hateful Herbert.

"They will, but..."

"And you've taken the day off work at the railway workshop. If you take another day they won't pay you. The manager might sack you. You'll starve."

Henri rubbed a hand over his smoke-stained brown hair. It stood up like a chimney-sweep's brush, only twice as sooty. "I don't know," he sighed.

"And your friends from the railway workshops are coming over before they start work. They'll push the airship to the Hippodrome racetrack. They'll be here any time now. They had to get out of bed

extra early. But they won't come again tomorrow."

"Perhaps."

"Here they are now. Oh, Mr Giffard, you have to fly today. You *have* to."

The man looked up at the sky where the winds whipped the ragged clouds towards the west. He stroked his bearded face and blinked. "Very well, I will fly."

Marie let out a low sigh that rattled the nests of the rats.

Chapter 3

It was ten o'clock before the monstrous balloon was in place on the open grass of the Hippodrome racetrack. The people of Paris had begun to gather. Some brought picnics – Marie watched with a watering mouth as the servants of a family of five

unloaded a basket from their carriage with a feast enough for fifty.

Their coachmen spread a rug on the grass and laid the plates and glasses and silver forks and spoons on the rug. Then they covered the plates in hams and sliced meats, fine white bread, and sauces and pickles and sweetmeats and fruits and salads.

There was a case full of wine that the children sipped with water, and lemon squashes and orange juices to cool them under the warm September sun.

Henri Giffard and his friends fanned the stove that filled the balloon with hot air while Marie picked up an old leather bucket with a poster on the side.

"It's a marvellous sight you're about to see," she cried to the crowd. "But Mr Giffard the inventor has spent every last sou on this marvellous airship."

She held up the bucket and rattled a few coins. "Give us your money. He hasn't enough money to even buy any lunch,"

she added as she began to drift towards the rich family at their picnic.

People began to drop money into her bucket. She noticed the poor gave more than the rich.

A boy about Marie's age wandered towards the fine feast. His clothes were fine – too fine for a boy with a ferret face. Stolen clothes, Marie guessed. His greedy, beady eyes darted from the food towards Marie's bucket with the growing collection of coins.

A small boy in a green velvet suit from the picnic family threw a chicken leg towards her. "Here, he can eat that," the boy said, and smirked as his family clapped their jewelled hands.

"Thank you, sir," Marie cried out loud. Then she quietly muttered, "I would like to thank you by shoving the bone down your fat little throat."

The father of the family called, "I say, girl. When does this thing go up? We can't wait forever."

"I'll ask," Marie offered. As she crossed towards the airship she murmured, "And I will take one of those plates to stick down *your* throat... your mouth is big enough. Idiot."

She took the food to Henri Giffard who was untangling the ropes that were holding a wood and wicker cabin below the air bag of the mighty ship. The wind caught the balloon as it rose and tugged at the heavy pegs that had been hammered into the grass.

As she handed him the chicken she asked, "Is everything going to work, Mr Giffard?"

"I don't think so," he groaned. "The balloon is filled with hydrogen gas. It will float. I don't see how I can feed the fire that powers the steam engine *and* work the sails that steer it. The airship needs *two* people to drive it."

One of the railway workers called across the cabin, "And he won't get one of us going up with him." He laughed. "We don't want to die."

"You're too heavy," the inventor shrugged.

Marie sighed. "Well, *I* would do it but I need to..."

"Perfect," the man with the sooty hair gasped. "Climb in, Marie."

"But the money..."

That was when the ferret-faced boy in the fine clothes stepped forward.

"Here, Miss, let me take that for you. I'll look after it if you want a little ride with the great man. Leave it with me."

Marie's eyes went narrow. "You'll steal it."

The boy's mouth fell open. "I would sooner steal my mother's wedding ring," he told her.

She began to shake her head, but Henri

Giffard cried out, "The pegs are breaking free. The airship will leave without us. Quickly, Marie!"

"Ohhhh," she cried and thrust the bucket into the hands of the boy. "Take it... collect as much as you can. We need every franc."

The ropes began to creak and sing in the wind. The inventor was already in the rising cabin and reached down to grasp Marie's hand. He pulled her up beside him.

The ferret-faced boy looked up and smiled. "I'll make a fortune, don't worry. I'll make a fortune."

With a crack and a slap, the last rope tore loose and the Giffard airship rose into the goose-grey September sky.

Chapter 4

The fire in the steam engine crackled and the wind moaned through the ropes as Marie and Henri rose above the crowds. All faces were turned up towards them like white daisies on the grass.

Marie felt a sudden sickness in her stomach as she looked down and turned towards the inventor.

"What do you want me to do?" she asked.

"When you pull that lever you open the needle valve and the propeller will start to turn," he said.

"That big wooden plank?" the girl frowned. "Plop-pillar?"

"Propeller... it *propels* us forward, see?"

"No."

"Just keep the fire box topped up with coal and push the lever to the right when I tell you," he said calmly. "You're a clever girl, Marie. You can do it."

No one had ever called her clever before and her heart swelled like the balloon above with pride.

"Yes, captain," she said with a cheeky grin and a mock salute.

The grimy streets of Paris drifted below and the Hippodrome racetrack was left behind as they drifted to the east. They followed the River Seine and its crowds of boats. Marie thought she could see the ocean far away.

"What if we end up in the sea?"

"I'll turn us round and take us back before that happens," the inventor said.

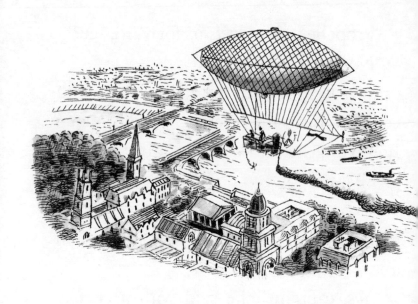

It was growing cold now as the dank clouds drifted across their open cabin. Marie huddled nearer the fire-box to stay warm.

"Lever to the right," the inventor cried. "Set the propeller going."

Marie swung the lever and watched open mouthed as steam hissed and spat and gurgled and whistled and the large blades began to turn.

Henri Giffard went to the rear of the cabin and grasped the ropes that would work the sail at the back.

"This is it, Marie. If this works we will be in the first airship ever to make its own way through the sky. Here goes..."

* * *

Ten thousand eyes followed the balloon over Paris. In the Hippodrome racetrack the crowds could still see it.

The rich family stopped chewing on their chicken and the father placed a spyglass to his eye.

"The propeller is turning," he said. "Now, let's see if it works... let's see if Giffard can bring his airship back against the wind."

The ferret-faced boy noticed that every face was turned up to the sky and took the

chance to slip some ham and cheeses into the secret, inside pockets of his coat. He would eat well that night.

He rattled the bucket that was half-full of coins now. "Give a few francs for a hero of France," he said in his most pleading and whining voice.

The man didn't take the spyglass from his eye but spoke quietly. "If that man can turn his airship around I'll give a *thousand* francs. France will be the first country in the world to build a real flying machine. We will all make our fortunes."

"So ten francs now will be no problem," the boy said and rattled again.

A coachman leaned forward and whispered in the boy's ear, "This is Mr Moulin. He has factories all over Paris. Your master will have a thousand francs if he turns that machine and sails against the wind."

"My master? Old Giffard isn't my master," the boy snorted.

"Then why are you collecting money for him?" the coachman asked sharply.

"Me? Er... a favour... yes, a favour for the girl." He laughed. "I'll hand over the money as soon as she lands," he lied.

"I don't believe you," Mr Moulin said.

"Five francs... two francs?" the boy wailed. "Give me two francs."

The factory owner kept his gaze on the balloon. "I will give you two policemen. One on each arm to march you off to jail."

"Jail? I've done nothing."

"You stole food from my family's picnic," the man replied in a voice as harsh as rusted iron.

"How did you – " the boy began. But a rumble like distant thunder grumbled across the Hippodrome racetrack as the

crowd began to murmur.

Mr Moulin jumped to his feet and cried,
"Look at that. Look at that..."

Chapter 5

"More coal in the fire-box," Henri Giffard shouted through the whipping wind.

The steam engine began to clatter like a beggar's bucket and the propeller turned

so fast it was a blur of wood. The whole cabin shook till Marie's teeth rattled in her head and her stomach jumped up to her throat.

She was staring straight ahead to the sea but then the whole airship began to groan and strain against the ropes that held it together. A startled seagull squawked and swerved close to the girl's face. When she looked again she wasn't looking at the sea. She was looking through the thin clouds towards the watery sun.

"The balloon has turned south," she gasped.

"Keep putting coal on the fire," Henri cried. "We're almost there."

When the girl looked up again she could see Paris below her again. "We've turned around," she said and jumped up and down on the creaking planks of the cabin. Even her dormouse weight made it rock a little and the floor tipped till she fell against the side. For a moment she found herself clinging to the side and looking down on the smoky roofs of the city.

The inventor grabbed her and pulled her back till she fell on the floor with a bump.

"Careful, girl. If you want to fly without the airship I'll throw you over the side.

Want that?" the man laughed, and his hair flew in the wind like a dark dandelion.

Marie grinned. "No, captain! But we did it, didn't we?"

The man shrugged again. "We are moving forward about ten kilometres an hour but the wind is fifteen kilometres an hour... really we're moving backwards. If we don't land soon, we'll be in the Bay of Biscay. I told you the wind was too strong to fly today, but you said we had to."

Marie pulled a face.

"Your landlord wanted the rent. He came at first light and said he'd tear the airship apart if you didn't pay by the end of the day. If you didn't fly today you never would."

The man's thin face was hollow and dark. "Ah, money," he said. "It isn't just the wind that's beaten me... it's my empty purse."

"The wind hasn't beaten you," Marie argued. "We can try again... on a calmer day we can fly to the moon and back. There will be money waiting when we land, just see. A bucket full of money."

But she knew in her heart it wasn't true.

The fabulous flyers made the balloon soar in circles over Paris as crowds cheered a thousand metres below them. Then, as the wind grew stronger, Henri shook his head. "We'll never make it back to the Hippodrome racetrack. Let's land where we can."

As he let the hydrogen gas out of the balloon they fell gently towards the district of Trappes, twenty-five kilometres away from their home.

Marie poured a bottle of water into the fire-box so there would be no sparks to turn them into a fireball, and they swooped down over houses towards a farm field full of cabbages.

The flyers held tight to the ropes as they hit the ground hard. The bag burst and let out the gas while the cabin turned to match-sticks and they were flung free. The cabbages saved them broken bones. The airship crumpled into a sad tangle of linen and firewood.

The farmer began to grumble about

crushed cabbages as he helped them from the wreckage but Marie spoke quickly.

"This airship is worth more than a few caterpillar-filled cabbages. He can keep it, can't he?" she asked the dazed inventor.

"It's no use to me," Henri Giffard said. "The linen alone cost me fifty francs – more than a month's wages in the railway workshops."

"And the steam motor?" the farmer asked.

The inventor looked as if he was going to argue but Marie looked at the cracked iron casing. "You can have that too... if you take us back to Paris in your cart."

And that was how the world's first fabulous flyers returned home that evening, sitting on a cart, chewing on cabbages.

They passed the Hippodrome racetrack they had left that morning. It was empty

now, apart from some dogs chasing rabbits and rats rooting among the left-over picnic crumbs. There was no crowd.

There was no boy with a bucket full of money.

The farmer's horse clopped along the cobbled road and the gloom of the evening was as deep as the gloom of the flyers.

Marie jumped down and ran to the door of the barn. Herbert the landlord waited, still wearing his tall top hat and still glaring with his weasel eyes. He held a shining key in his hand.

"Let us in, Mr Herbert," she pleaded.

He shook his head slowly. "Remember what we agreed? Fifty francs or out you go."

"We don't have fifty francs," Marie mumbled.

"Then out you go," Herbert laughed.
"Get back to the gutter where you belong."

Chapter 6

The gas-lamps in the street flared into a greenish glow as the gas-lighter man turned them on with his pole. The light turned the pale faces of Marie and Henri Giffard a grim and ghostly shade.

"My tools are in the building," the inventor said quietly.

Herbert grinned and said, "Good. I will sell them to pay the twenty-franc rent you owe me."

"I need the tools for my job at the railway workshop," Henri Giffard said.

"You shouldn't have wasted all your money on that silly balloon, then," Herbert sneered.

Marie walked over to the landlord and clutched at his waistcoat. "Oh, good sir, would you see us out on the streets, penniless and starving?"

"Yes," the man replied.

Marie nodded and walked away. No one heard her mutter, "Then it serves you right that I just nicked your watch and chain."

As she began to tug at the inventor's sleeve there came a harsh clatter of iron-tyred wheels and horse's hooves that sparked and screeched round the cobblestone corner.

The landlord stumbled out of the way of the carriage as the driver reined in the

horses, threw on the brake and skidded to a stop.

"Murdering maniac," Herbert roared. "Your master should take your horsewhip and use it on you."

A voice said, "I am his master," and the carriage door opened. Mr Moulin, the factory owner, stepped down. "You are?"

The landlord seemed to shrink and cower.

"Oh, sir, what an honour to see you in this part of Paris. An honour."

Moulin strode past him and grasped Henri Giffard's hand.

"I saw your display today, my man. Brilliant, quite amazing. I want to work with you to make even better airships."

"Work *with* him?" Marie laughed. "You don't want to get those posh clothes dirty."

Moulin shook his head. "No, no. I supply the money and give you a place to work. Is this your workshop?" he asked and nodded towards the long and shabby barn. "I'm sure we can find somewhere better."

"No," the landlord groaned. "This is a wonderful workshop. The best. Better than the best. Good enough for my hero, Henri Giffard."

"It's full of rats," Marie argued.

"I'll clear them out myself tomorrow. And I'll forget about the little matter of the fifty francs you owe for rent."

"Twenty francs," the girl reminded him.

"Twenty, then. Just say you'll stay. I would love to do business with Mr Moulin. Love it."

The inventor and the factory owner looked at one another.

"We can talk about it at dinner tonight," Moulin said. "Let me take you to a fine hotel where they serve the best food in Paris."

"Can I come?" Marie asked. "I helped the captain sail the ship through the air."

"Of course," the factory owner said. "Let me help you into my carriage."

Marie smiled. "One moment," she said.

She crossed the cobbles to where the landlord stood in humble silence. "I have a present for you, Mr Herbert," she said.

"For me?"

"For you. Close your eyes."

He did as she said. She slipped his watch into his pocket. "Open them."

"What is it?" he asked, baffled.

The girl ran to the carriage and Mr Moulin helped her onto the fine velvet seat.

"You'll never know," Marie called to the landlord. "You'll never know." She waved through the carriage window as the horse trotted away. "Sorry, Mr Herbert, I simply must fly."

True History

Henri Gifford invented the first powered airship. The hydrogen-balloon airship had a steam engine that drove a propeller.

On 24 September 1852 Giffard made the first powered and controlled flight travelling over 25 km from Paris to Trappes. The wind was too strong to allow him to make way against it, so he was unable to return to the start. But he was able to make turns and circles, showing that a powered airship could be steered and could fly anywhere on a calm day.

Henri worked on the French railways and made very little money. The cost of building his first airship left him poor. His inventions started to make him money and he used it to build a second airship. That didn't work so well and it crashed.

Thirty years after his fabulous first flight he started to go blind. He couldn't bear it so he killed himself.

The famous Eiffel Tower was built in 1889. On the tower there are 72 names carved: the names of 72 people who made France great. Henri Giffard's name is there.

You try

1. Eilmer was a monk around a thousand years ago. When he was a boy he read the old Greek story of Daedalus.

Can you use the internet to find out what happened to Daedalus and then tell the story to a friend?

2. Eilmer believed HE could build

a flying machine. Another monk
wrote what happened next...

*Eilmer fastened wings to his hands
and feet and waited for a breeze at
the top of a church tower. He flew
for more than a furlong [200 metres].*

*But stirred by the force of the
wind and the swirling of air, he
fell, broke both his legs and was
lame ever after.*

Can YOU design a flying machine
that would work better than
Eilmer's? You could make a model.
Just DON'T try to fly yourself.

3. Mr Henri Giffard's poster said he would fly the first powered air machine in history. He wanted thousands of people to come and see him. Could you draw a poster with great words and pictures that would make everyone want to see that first flight?

Tudor Tales

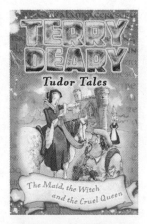

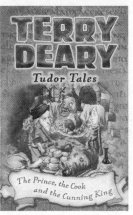

Exciting, funny stories based on real events...
welcome to the Tudor times!

Egyptian Tales

Exciting, funny stories based on real events...
welcome to ancient Egypt!

Terry Deary's Shakespeare Tales

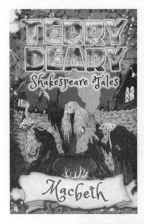

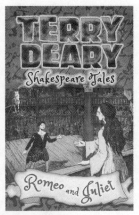

If you liked this book
why not look out for the rest of
Terry Deary's Shakespeare Tales?
Meet Shakespeare and his
theatre company!

World War II Tales

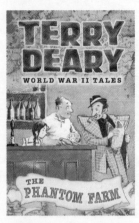

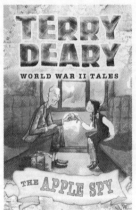

Exciting, funny stories based on real events...
welcome to World War II!